NAJIM ZAFIR'S

hassas

#١

CREATIVE DIRECTOR
NAJIM ZAFIR

COVER BY: COLORS BY: ART BY:
KOMI OLAF   SAM DELA TORRE   ELTON THOMASI   VICTOR FORSON
                                PAGES 1-11,13   PAGES 12,14-18

Najim Zafir Inc   www.MistryKIDD.blogspot.com   www.MistryKIDD.wordpress.com

AT THE HEART OF THE PARTY, THE KING
DOESN'T LET HIS POSITION RUIN HIS FUN.
WITH A BOULDER ON HIS SHOULDER
SO HE PICKS THEM OFF
SPRAY VENOM ON OUR ENEMIES SPIT THEM OFF
I NEVER MISS WHEN I DISS-MISS KISS THE FALL
BUT NO DROPPING OUT I STILL RIP UP BARZ
HIP, HIP, HOP STAR
BEH
BEH-BEH
BEST OF ALL
NO ONE DISRESPECTS THE GODZ
FROM THEM WE ALL COME
AND TO THEM WE RETURN
SO DANCE FOR YOUR LIFE
YOU SHOULD
DO IT FOR YOU
DANCE FOR YOUR KING
JUST SAY
YOU DID IT FOR HIM

DRINK FOR THE NIGHT
GO ON
YOU SHOULD
DO IT FOR YOU
DANCE FOR YOUR LIFE
COME ON
DO IT FOR YOU
SING FOR THE GODS
GO ON
YOU SHOULD
DO IT FOR YOU!!!
FOR THE FAMILY!!!!!!!!!!!!!

SPEAK!
WHILE YOU STILL HAVE A VOICE
THERE'S NO POINT HOLDING OUT. YOUR CHOICES ARE LIMITED
PLEASE, YOU NEED TO BELIEVE ME.
LYING WILL ONLY HURT YOU FURTHER
I KNOW NOTHING. I SWEAR! THIS IS ALL A MISTA...
THE MISTAKE IS YOURS I'M AFRAID
KOFF!! KOFF!! KAKK!
PLEASE YOUR MAJESTY. YOU HAVE TO BELIEVE ME. I DIDN'T KNOW! I DON'T KNOW ANYTHING!
I SWEAR TO YOU!!!
YOU CAN NOT SWEAR AND THEN BARE FALSE TESTIMONY YOU HEATHEN
HAVE SOME DIGNITY, AT LEAST GIVEN YOUR CURRENT POSITION
KOFF!! KOFF!!
WHA...?

FROM OUTSIDE, IT LOOKS LIKE ANY OTHER HUT. FAR AWAY FROM THE WALLS OF THE FOREST KING CITY.
MY KING, I THINK I'VE OUTSTAYED MY USEFULNESS. THE EXCITEMENT EXCEEDS ME.
HAVE A HORSE READY FOR..
I WOULD RATHER WALK WITH ALI MANN FATHER. I NEED SOME NIGHT TIME AIR IN MY LUNGS
VERY WELL. ALI MANN, TAKE MY PRINCE BACK TO HIS QUARTERS IN THE CITY. BE ON FULL ALERT! WE CAN NEVER BE SURE GIVEN TONIGHTS INCIDENT. CHECK ON YOUR BROTHER AS WELL.
CANT BELIEVE WHAT'S HAPPENING
MY FATHER. BELOVED KING OF THE WESTERNERS. THE FOREST LANDS. THE GREEN KINGDOM.
TO BE ATTACKED WITHIN HIS WALLS? ON A CELEBRATION OF HIS LIFE?
CAN THERE BE MORE TO COME?
ARE WE WELL PREPARED?
WHO CAN WE TRUST?

14

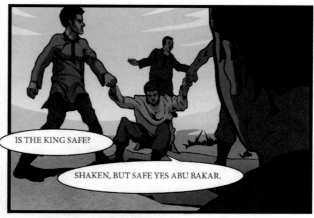

NAJIM ZAFIR'S

hassas

#2

CREATIVE DIRECTOR
NAJIM ZAFIR

ART BY:

ELTON THOMASI
PAGES 1,7,8, 11-18

VICTOR FORSON
PAGES 2-6,9,10

COLORS BY:
SAM DELA TORRE

COVER BY:
SAM DELA TORRE

Najim Zafir Inc   www.MistryKiDD.blogspot.com   www.MistryKiDD.wordpress.com

It's PARTY TIME!
ON THE EAST SIDE!!!!

THIS VIEW, PEACEFUL AS IT MAY BE IS MERELY A FOLLICLE OF THE ELEGANCE THAT IS THE EASTERN KINGDOM.

BUT BEFORE WE GET INTO ALL THE FESTIVITIES,

LET'S AT LEAST KNOW WHY WE ARE CELEBRATING.

ABI?*
MAKES SENSE RIGHT?
I THOUGHT SO TOO

*ABI= right

THE RIVER KINGDOMS.
HOME TO THE FISHERS, DIVERS,
BOAT BUILDERS & RIDERS.

20

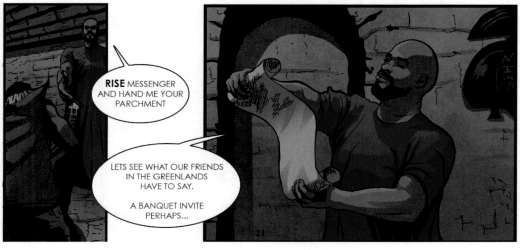

INDEED...

YOU MAY TAKE YOUR LEAVE MESSENGER

King Kunlay of The River Kingdom,

I and a small party shall arrive at your gates shortly

I hope the whispers of your wisdom are not exaggerated
A resolution not met could be unfavourable

King Obinok of the Western Land, Protector of The Forests

READ THIS PLEASE *ADVISOR DOSU*. I MAY NO LONGER HAVE THAT ABILITY IT SEEMS.

WITH HASTE GOOD SIR!

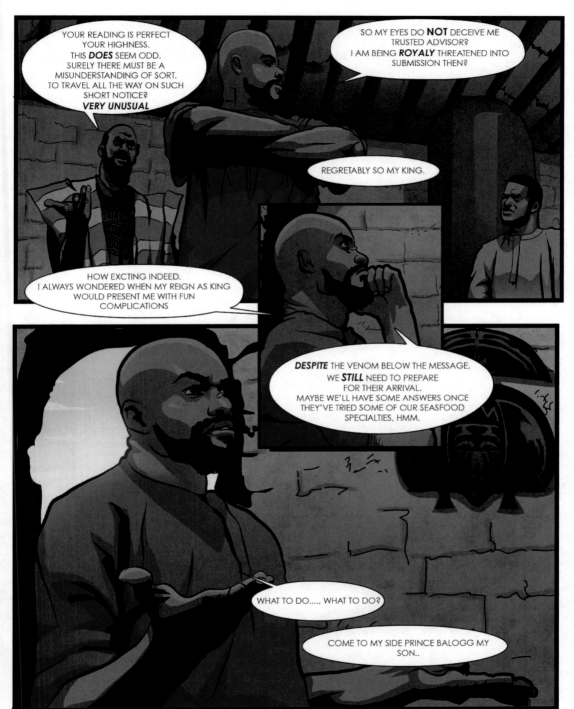

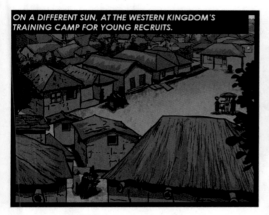

ON A DIFFERENT SUN, AT THE WESTERN KINGDOM'S TRAINING CAMP FOR YOUNG RECRUITS.

CHUWA (RECRUIT TRAINER): DO I LOOK LIKE YOUR MOTHER? *THROW THAT PUNCH LIKE IT DID SOMETHING TO YOU!*

LEFT KICK!

RIGHT KICK!

LEFT PUNCH!

KICK HIGHER TORTOISE!!

RIGHT PUNCH!

LAHI. I'M WATCHING YOU! DON'T MAKE ME COME AND SHOW YOU HOW TO THROW *A REAL PUNCH!!!*

AND NOW. A NEW COMBINATION! *WATCH ME!*

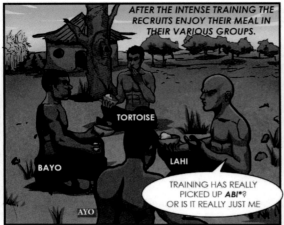

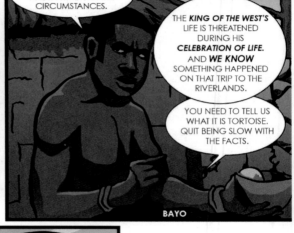

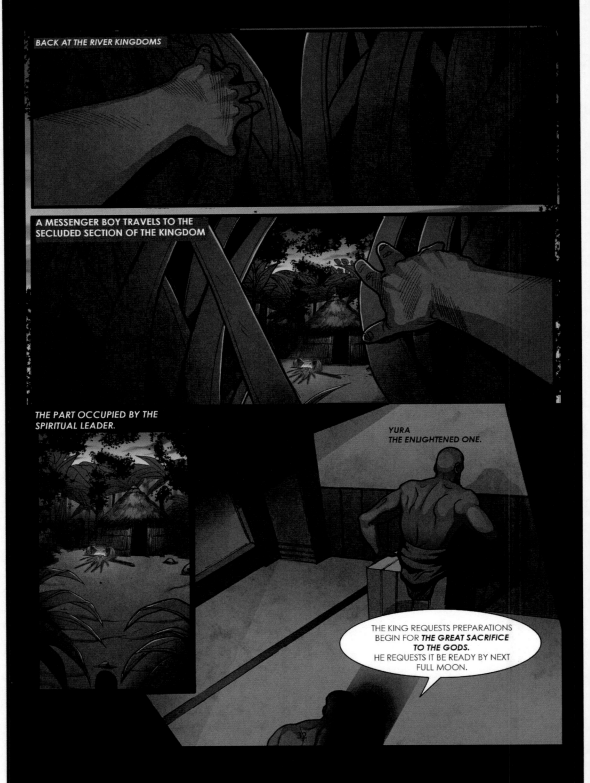

AND AT A SAFER LOCATION IN THE RIVER KINGDOM.
CAVE OLOBIRI TO BE EXACT.
CONSIDERED A CENTRE OF SPIRITUAL IMPORTANCE TO
THE RIVERLAND PEOPLE.

WE JOIN THE YEARLY SACRIFICE FOR THE GODS.
A NIGHT OF WORSHIP.

AND OF COURSE
CELEBRATION

LOOK!
THE ROYAL FAMILY.
THEY'RE HERE!

PRINCE BALOGG   KING KUNLAY

THE CEREMONY DOESN'T BEGIN UNTIL THE KING ARRIVES.
HE AND HIS FAMILY PRAY AT HOME BEFORE JOINING THE REST OF THE KINGDOM.

THE ROYAL WOMEN ARE ADVISED TO STAY HOME AND PRAY FROM THERE.

MEMBERS OF ALL THE NEIGHBORING TRIBES CONTRIBUTE THEIR OFFERINGS TO THE GODS.
FOODSTUFF, LIVESTOCK, & THINGS THEY MADE THEMSELVES.
EVERYTHING IS GATHERED OVER MOONS AND PRESENTED COMMUNALLY.

NOW THE ROYAL MEN ARE HERE, IT IS TIME.

BUT BACK IN THE FOREST
WATCH!
OU..!
GET THOSE HORSES TO CALM DOWN!
WE NEED TO ASK YOU SOME QUESTIONS ....
PRINCE BALOGG.
WE KNOW ITS YOU.

NAJIM ZAFIR'S

hassan

#٤

CREATIVE DIRECTOR
NAJIM ZAFIR

ART BY:
ELTON THOMASI

COLORS BY:
SAM DELA TORRE

COVER BY:
SAM DELA TORRE

AND YOU SIR? WHY ARE WE ALL GATHERED HERE TODAY IN HOLY UNITY
AS THE YOUNG LADY SAID, TO HONOR THE GODS.
TO HONOR THE GODS, YES. BUT WHAT ABOUT THE ENLIGHTENED ONES WHO WERE STOLEN FROM US MANY MANY MOONS AGO?
AN ACT OF HATRED. AN ACT OF EVIL. AN ACT OF WAR EVEN.
YET WE REPAY THAT BLOOD SPILT WITH PEACE AND HONOR.

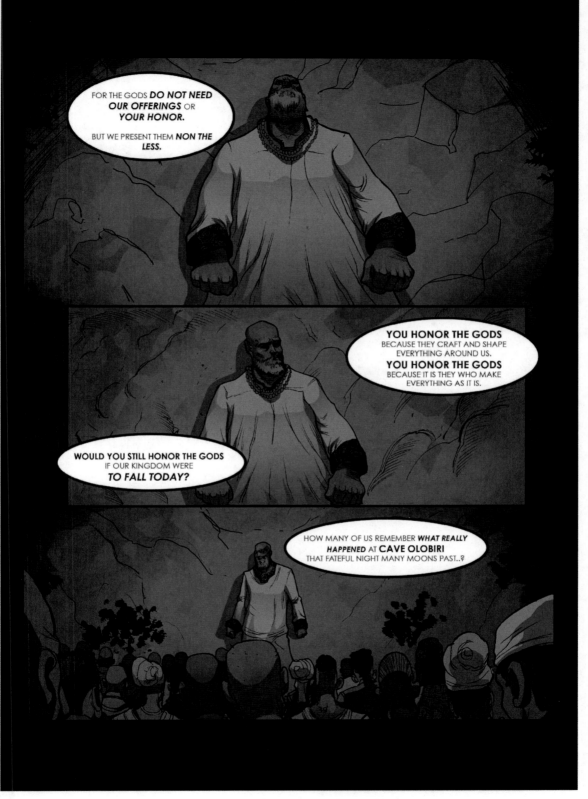

MY KING, PLEASE STAY CLOSE.
WE ARE LOSING THE LIGHT AND MAY BE A DISTANCE FROM THE CITY
MY SON MUST BE FOUND. ALL OTHER CONSIDERATIONS ARE NON-EXISTENT
OF COURSE SIRE!
ONWARDS!

THE CONNECTIONS BETWEEN SEEMINGLY UNRELATED EVENTS CAN NOT BE OVERLOOKED.
THE ATROCITIES THAT WERE ENACTED UPON OUR ENLIGHTENED ONES WITHIN THESE VERY WALLS..
THINGS THAT CAN NEVER BE FORGOTTEN.
NOR SHOULD THEY EVER BE.
LIFE WAS SACRIFIED HERE.
LIFE WE STRIVE TO HONOR
LIFE WE STRIVE TO REKINDLE.

WHERE DOES *LIFE TAKE YOU?*

WHEN *THOSE WHO BROUGHT YOU* HERE

END UP *LEAVING* YOU, WHETHER *BY CHOICE OR NOT*

NOT BEFORE NAMING ME *JOY* OF COURSE

AYO MEANS JOY

YOUR GRANDMOTHER HAS TO BE A MOTHER ALL OVER AGAIN

AND WHEN SHE'S HAD ENOUGH, AN AUNTY DOES HER BEST

TILL SHE CANT ANYMORE EITHER

WHEN LEFT ALONE, YOU HAVE TO MAKE YOURSELF USEFUL.

MAKE YOURSELF *NEEDED.* THAT MEANS DOING *WHATEVER IS NEEDED.*

WHATEVER THAT MIGHT BE

QUICKLY!
UNMASK HIM SO WE MAY CONTINUE OUR INTERROGATION
THERE'S A PROBLEM CAPTAIN.
WHAT NOW?!
HE DOESN'T FIT THE DESCRIPTION WE WERE GIVEN.
THATS BECAUSE HE ISN'T THE PRINCE. WE'VE BEING DECEIVED. SOMEHEOW, THEY WERE EXPECTING US
WE HAVE TO KILL THEM ALL.
WOLE, TAKE CHARGE. MAKE IT LOOK LIKE A VIOLENT ROBBERY

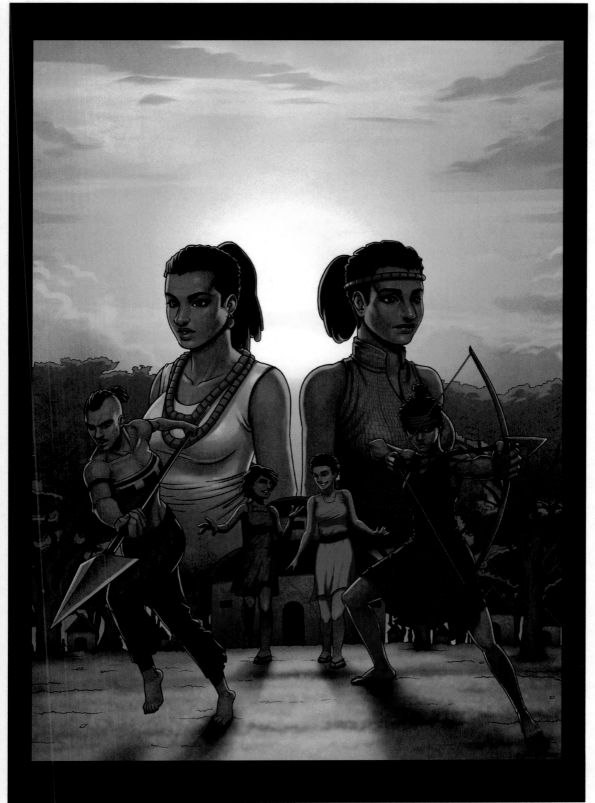

NAJIM ZAFIR'S
hassa ﻊﻤﻌﻳ
4

CREATIVE DIRECTOR
NAJIM ZAFIR

COLORS BY: ART BY: COVER BY:

SAM DELA TORRE   **HERO DELA TORRE**   **SAM DELA TORRE**

PG 1-5, 15
ELTON THOMASI

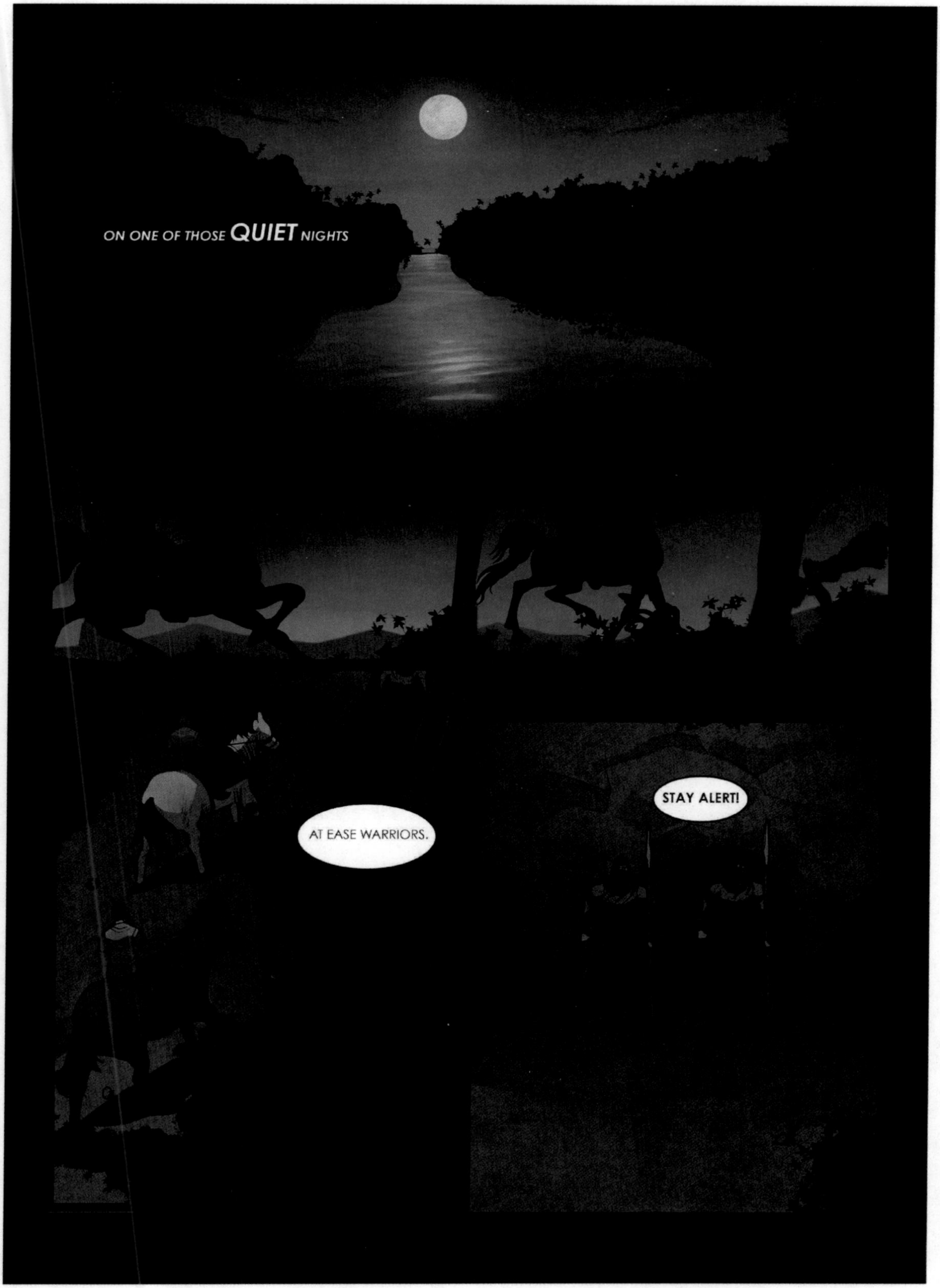
ON ONE OF THOSE QUIET NIGHTS
AT EASE WARRIORS.
STAY ALERT!

IN A MORE QUIET
PART OF THE WOODS
THINGS ARE GETTING REALLY TIGHT AROUND HERE.
ESPECIALLY AFTER THAT LAST INCIDENT.* THEY ARE GOING TO FIGURE IT OUT. VERY SOON
IT'S ALMOST TIME MY PET. DON'T WORRY TOO MUCH.
WHY DON'T WE LEAVE TOGETHER LIKE I KEEP PROPOSING...
SHHH... DONT SAY ANYMORE...
*ISSUE #3

THE FOREST KINGDOM
ROYAL QUARTERS
I HONESTLY HAVEN'T SEEN **ANYONE** THAT HAS THE TALENT OF **WOLE**
I KNOW HE SEEMS TO BE GOOD AT **EVERYTHING.**
HE MAY ACTUALLY BE ABLE TO BEAT THE BEST IN **MY KINGDOM**
SHOOO. PRINCESS, ARE YOU FALLING JUST A LITTLE BIT?
MAYBE A **LITTLE LITTLE BIT.** BUT **I PROMISE,** YOU WILL DIE A SLOW DEATH IF YOU REPEAT TO **ANYONE**
YOU KNOW I'M YOUR GIRL. YOU CAN COUNT ON ME PRINCESS

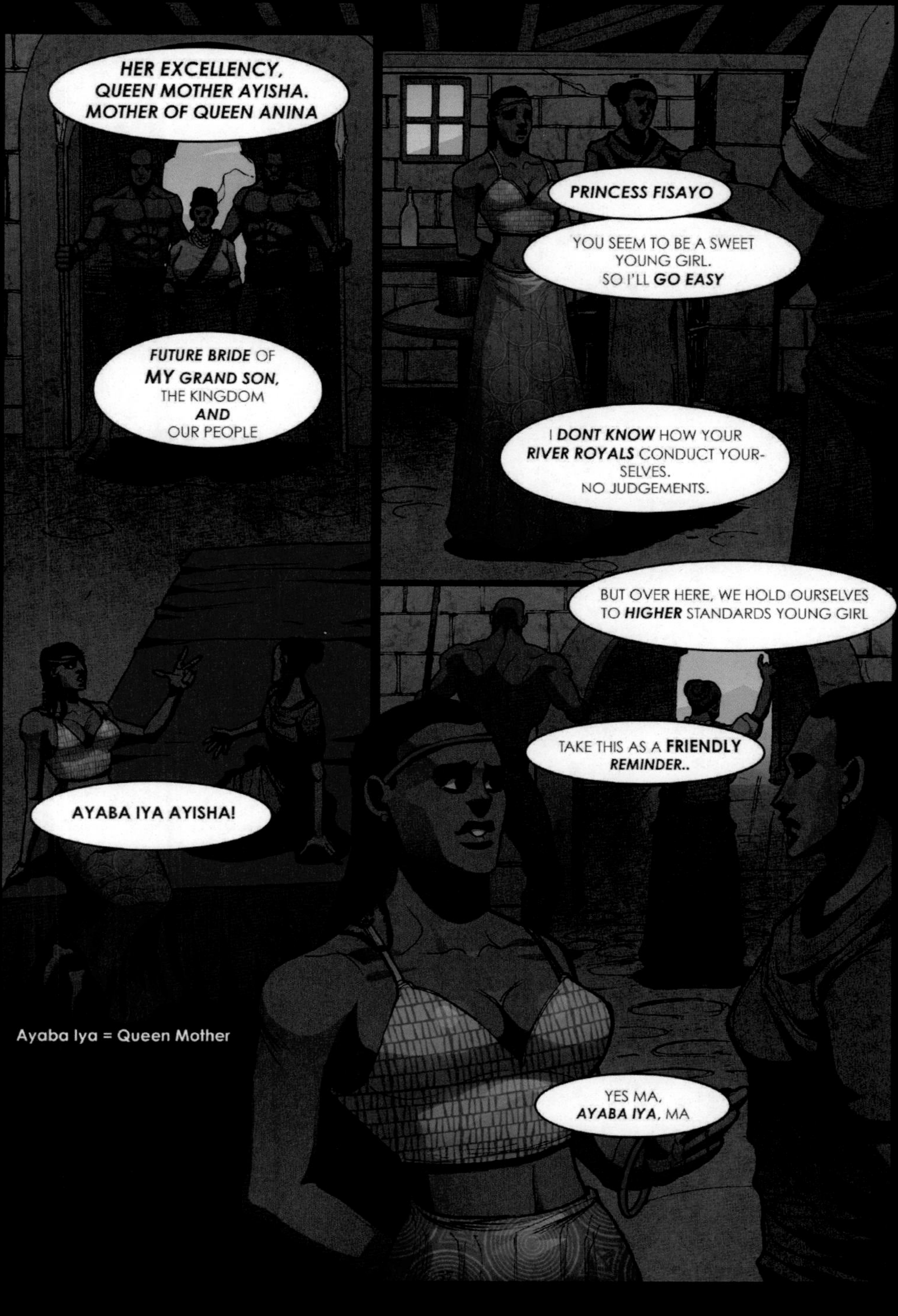

Ayaba Iya = Queen Mother

IT'S **NEW ARRIVALS** DAY
AT THE RIVER KINGDOM

WELCOME!
WELCOME TO KING CITY!!
I'M MOYA, YOUR GUIDE
FOR THE DAY.

THIS IS *AUNTY MORA*.
SHE HEADS THE WOMEN
TOWN OF KING CITY, SO
MAKE SURE YOU'RE NICE

DOWN THESE HALLS IS WHERE THE
NEW GIRLS STAY.
WHEN YOUR ROLE HAS BEEN SET YOU
MOVE AROUND TO THE VARIOUS
GROUP HOUSES

SOME OF YOU WILL BE FISHERS,
ARCHERS, CRAFTERS, OR EVEN
WARRIORS

HOW EXCITING!

AND THIS IS YOUR ROOM.
SETTLE IN, AND YOU'LL BE SENT FOR
SHORTLY.

58

MORE PRESSING ISSUES

YOUR HIGHNESS,
KING OBINOK
DID NOT ARRIVE LIKE HIS
SCROLL SAID HE WOULD*

HE DIDN'T SEEM HAPPY THEN,
WE CAN ONLY ASSUME
BY HIS ABSENCE..

*ISSUE #2

..AND LACK OF FURTHER
CONTACT,...

HIS MOOD HASN'T IMPROVED.

WELL OBSERVED ADVISOR DOSU.
SOMETHING CHANGED HIS MIND
ABOUT THE VISIT

DO YOU HAVE ANY IDEAS
HOW TO PROCEED?

A FEW SIRE..

THE NEW RIVER GIRLS'
FIRST MEAL

THE GIRLS IN THE **FOREST KINGDOM** TALK **PROSPECTS**

CAN ANYONE REALLY TAKE OUT WOLE?

IT'S NOT EVEN FAIR.

I THINK TORTOISE WILL SURPRISE US

WHAT! YOU'RE SMOKING SOME WILD BUSHES **ABI**? ONLY PERSON WORSE IS **NAJIM!**

Z<GIGGLES>Z

AFTER THE MEAL THE **NEW RIVER GIRLS** TALK **EXPERIENCE**

I'VE NEVER...

THOUGHT ABOUT IT...

ME NEITHER...

I CERTAINLY HAVE.

MANY TIMES!

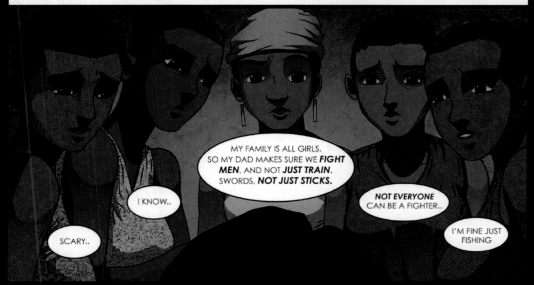

MY FAMILY IS ALL GIRLS. SO MY DAD MAKES SURE WE **FIGHT MEN**, AND NOT **JUST TRAIN**. SWORDS, **NOT JUST STICKS.**

I KNOW..

SCARY..

NOT EVERYONE CAN BE A FIGHTER..

I'M FINE JUST FISHING

....AND MAY THE GODS BLESS THIS FAMILY AND THE MEAL WE ARE ABOUT TO ENJOY

MY SWEET SWEET DAUGHTERS, WHO IS ON SOUP DUTY TODAY?

CHICHI!

CHICHI!

CHI!

CHICHI!

HUSBAND, PLEASE TAKE IT EASY ON HER. SHE IS VERY BUSY GETTING READY FOR HER KING CITY APPLICATION

MY SWEET BEAUTIFUL BRIDE, YOU ARE LOVING TO A FAULT..

THOUGHT I'D BE HAPPY AWAY BUT I FEEL EVEN WORSE NOW

COURT OF KING KUNLAY

OUR GREAT KING KUNLAY HAS DECLARED ALL PEOPLE OF COMBAT SKILL

REPORT TO THEIR VARIOUS GROUP LEADERS

DELIVER THIS TO ALL THE QUARTERS IN KING CITY.

ALL ABLE BODIED PERSONS...

SPREAD THE WORD

65

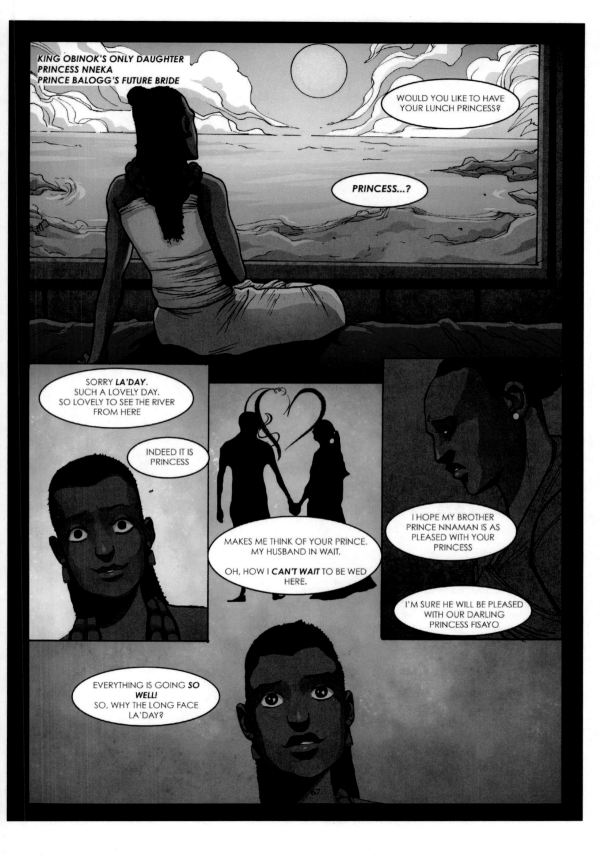

NAJIM ZAFIR'S

hassan

#5

CREATIVE DIRECTOR
NAJIM ZAFIR

COLORS BY:
SAM DELA TORRE

ART BY:
ELTON THOMASI

COVER BY:
SAM DELA TORRE

AYO and BAYO

...FOR THE LAST TIME AYO, IF YOU'RE SCARED WE CAN TRY ANOTHER SECTION

WHERE DID YOU HEAR "SCARED" YOU *MUMU!* I'M ASKING IF YOU'RE SURE WHERE WE'RE **GOING!?**

IT'S TOO DARK TO BE WALKING AROUND THE FOREST BLINDLY...

SEE! SHED SKIN, WE ARE DEFINITELY ON THE RIGHT TRACK.

STEADY...

SLOWLY....

........GODS ABOVE.....

I'M SEEING MOVEMENT .. IN THE TREES...

AT A DIFFERENT PART OF THE FOREST
WOLE AND OYE HAVE BEEN TRACKING A
PRIDE OF LIONS NOW LEAVING FOR A HUNT

THE PRIDE MAKES ITS WAY PAST OUR RECRUITS
WHO ARE DOING ALL THEY CAN TO STAY HIDDEN
AND UNDETECTED

SO BEGINS THEIR HUNT FOR THE NIGHT

"ALRIGHT OYE LET'S ROLL.
WE DON'T WANT TO LOSE THEM."
SOFTLY SPOKEN BUT WITH URGENCY

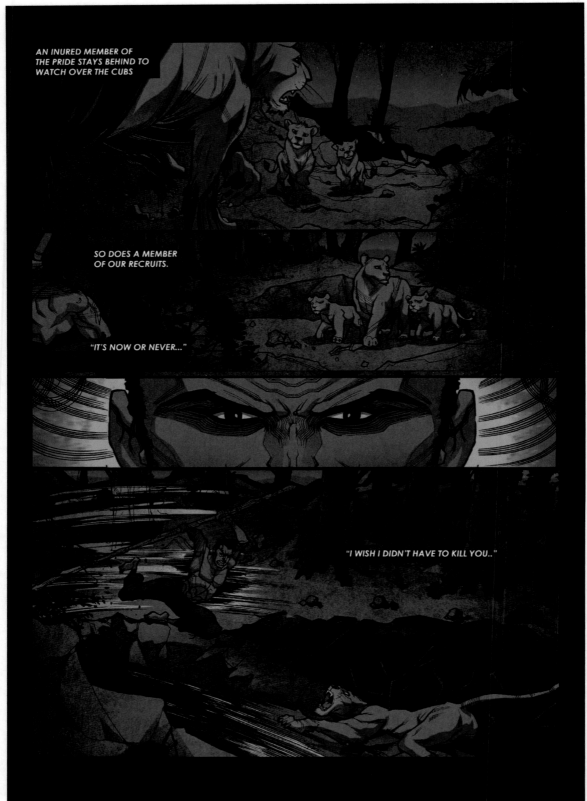

IN...
COMING...
SPLIT!
WE MUST CONFUSE IT SOMEHOW!
I'M OPEN TO ANY IDEAS...

"WHICH JUST NEVER LASTS..."

"WE MUST"

"TAKE"

"OUR MOMENT"

"NOT LET IT GO"

THE REST OF THE PRIDE GOES ON THE CHASE
AFTER CHECKING ON HIM

"OUR MOMENT"

MAGGOTS
INVALIDS
THAT'S WHAT YOU HAVE BEEN
IS THAT ALL YOU WILL BE? THAT'S WHAT WE WILL FIND OUT
CAN ANY OF YOU CONQUER NATURE?
CAN ANY OF YOU CONNECT WITH NATURE?
OR WILL YOU SIMPLY BE FOOD FOR THE FOREST SOIL AND IT'S ANIMALS?
WE'LL SEE WHEN YOU RETURN
IF YOU DO

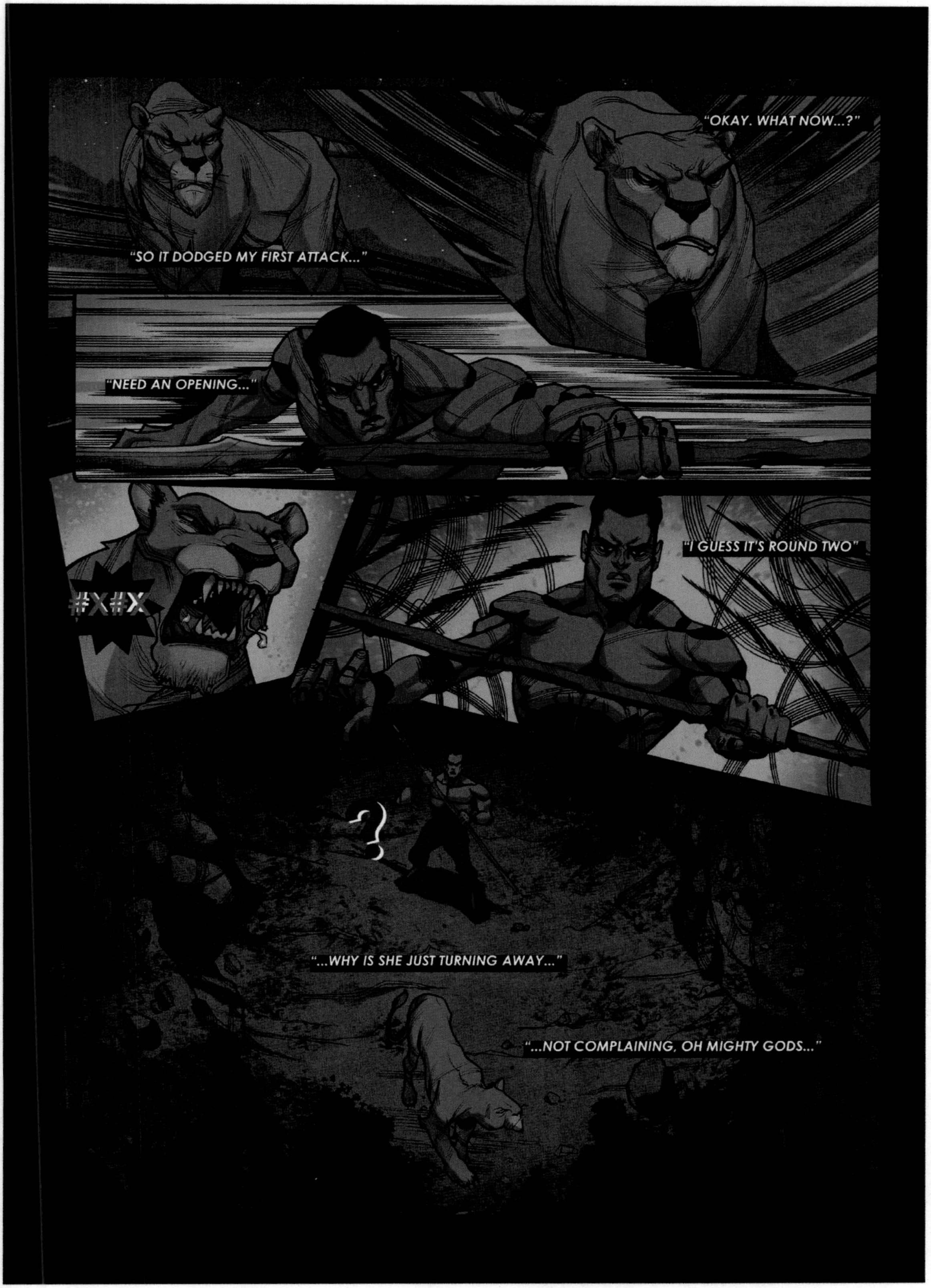
"SO IT DODGED MY FIRST ATTACK..."
"OKAY. WHAT NOW...?"
"NEED AN OPENING..."
#X#X
"I GUESS IT'S ROUND TWO"
?
"...WHY IS SHE JUST TURNING AWAY..."
"...NOT COMPLAINING, OH MIGHTY GODS..."

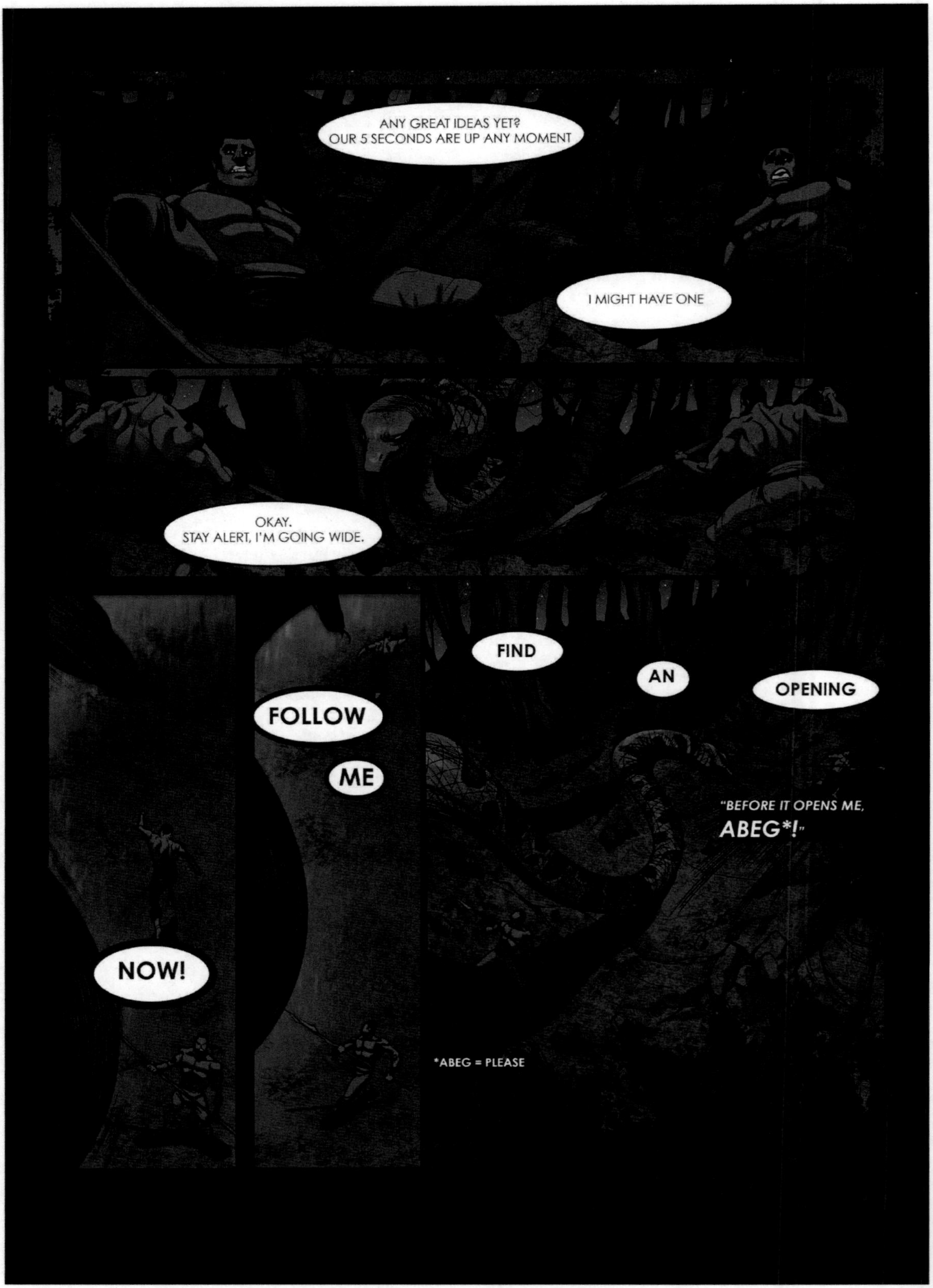
ANY GREAT IDEAS YET? OUR 5 SECONDS ARE UP ANY MOMENT
I MIGHT HAVE ONE
OKAY. STAY ALERT, I'M GOING WIDE.
NOW!
FOLLOW
ME
FIND
AN
OPENING
"BEFORE IT OPENS ME, ABEG*!"
*ABEG = PLEASE

"OUR MOMENT TO SUBDUE THE STRAGGLER"
WE HAVE TO END THIS
BEFORE HIS PRIDE RETURNS FOR HIM.
TOO LATE...
XRRRRX
XRRRRX
XRRRRX

80

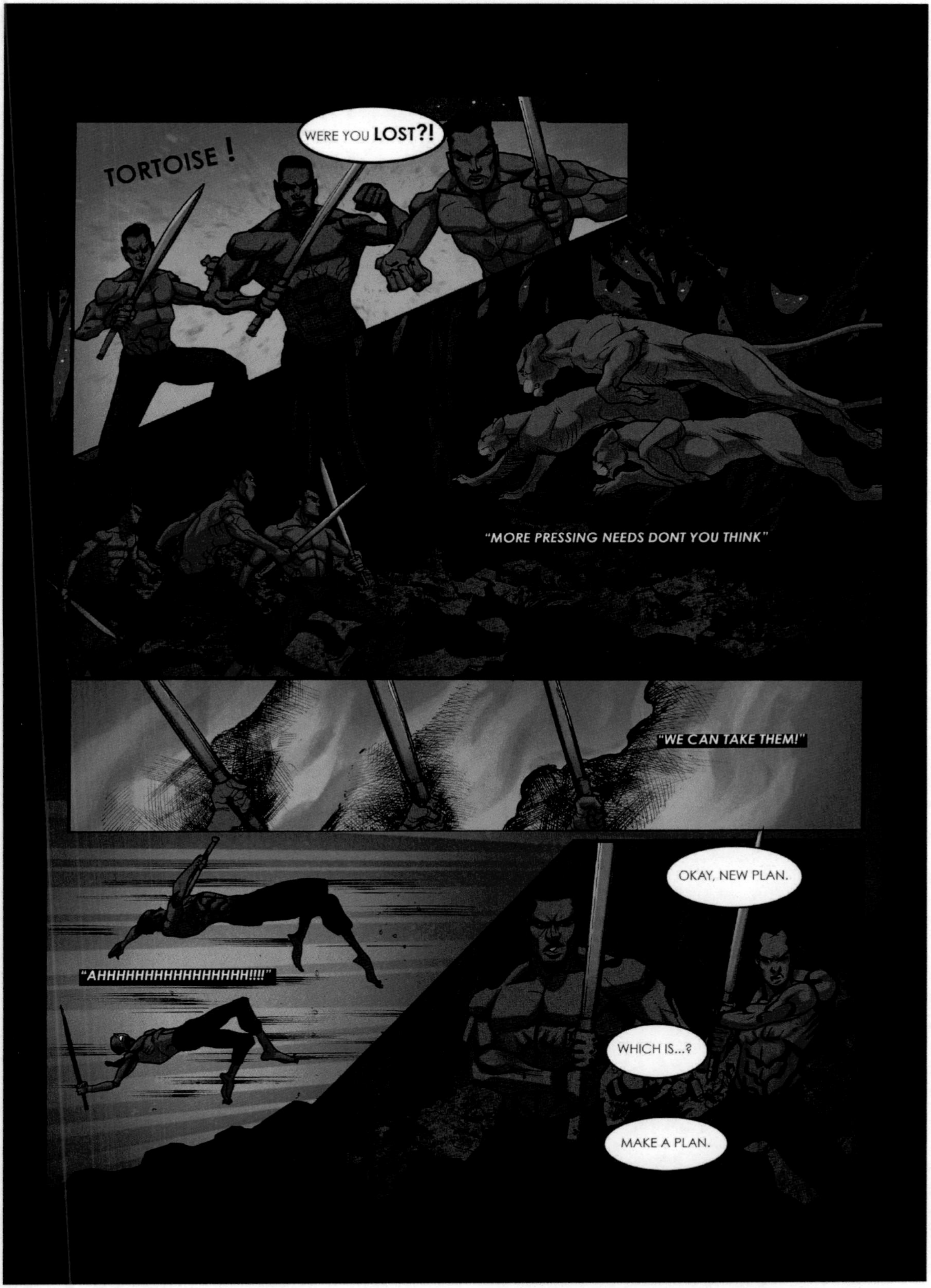

TORTOISE !
WERE YOU LOST?!
"MORE PRESSING NEEDS DONT YOU THINK"
"WE CAN TAKE THEM!"
"AHHHHHHHHHHHHHHHH!!!!"
OKAY, NEW PLAN.
WHICH IS...?
MAKE A PLAN.

ON THE VERY SAME NIGHT
IN THE VERY SAME FOREST
THE VERY SAME TEST
"DEAR GODS!"
"AFTER WAITING SO LONG, IT'S SPOTTED ME"
#X#X
"NO TIME TO THINK!"
"IT'S COMING FOR ME!"

"I WISH THIS WEREN'T SO"
"I DO NOT WISH TO HARM YOU"
"GRACIOUS ONE"
"BUT I ALSO WISH TO LIVE"
"THE MOMENT"
"STILL ALIVE!"
"WHAT'S NEXT.."
"GRACIOUS ONE?"

NAJIM ZAFIR'S

6

CREATIVE DIRECTOR
NAJIM ZAFIR

COLORS BY:
SAM DELA TORRE

ART BY:
HERO DELA TORRE

COVER BY:
SAM DELA TORRE

MADAME MORENE AND THE ENLIGHTENED ONES OF THE FOREST KINGDOM, IN PRAYER
"......................"
"..............."
HIM...???
REALLY???

THE RIVER KINGDOM: KING KUNLAY'S COURT
MY KING, I REALLY BELIEVE WITH THE CURRENT TENSION
A MEASURED APPROACH MIGHT BE BEST.
WE DON'T WANT TO RUSH TO ANY DECISIONS, JUST YET
ADVISOR DOSU, THEY HAVE HEARD WE ATTACKED KING OBINOK AND HIS MEN. TWICE!
THEY BELIEVE WE ARE RESPONSIBLE, SO WE MUST DECIDE QUICK
AND ACT QUICKER.
I THINK, YOUR HIGHNESS...
WE MUST PREPARE FOR RETALIATION.
THE MESSAGE IN THE CARE OF THIS RIDER HOLDS THE DIFFERENCE BETWEEN PEACE AND UNREST

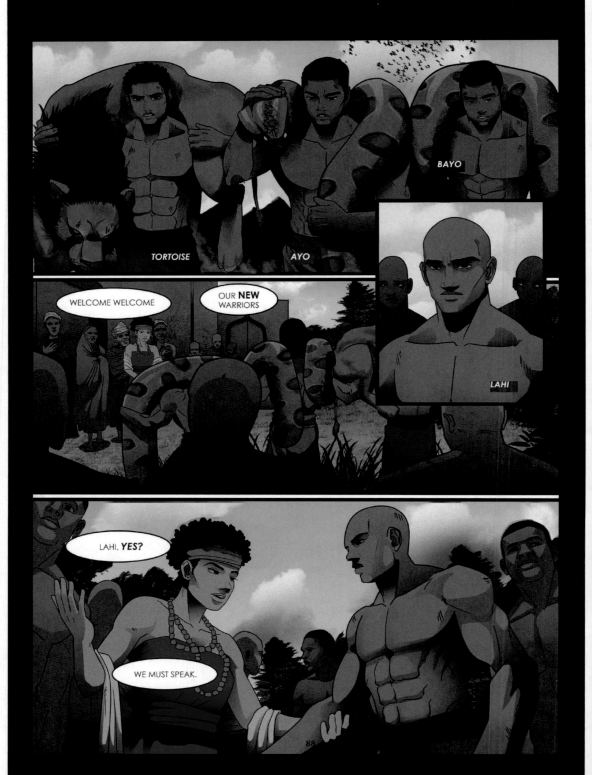

KING OBINOK RETIRES TO A CHAMBER TO MEET WITH TODAY'S GUESTS
PROTECTOR OF THE FOREST KINGDOMS, KING OBINOK
PROTECTOR OF THE FOREST KINGDOMS, KING OBINOK
I WISH I HAD BETTER NEWS, BUT MY WIVES TELL ME THE TALK OF UNREST FROM THE RIVER KINGDOMS IS GETTING LOUDER
MY NEWS ISN'T BETTER MY KING, I'M SORRY TO SAY. PEOPLE CAN FEEL SOMETHING IS BUILDING
PERHAPS SOME SORT OF GESTURE OF GOODWILL TOWARDS THE RIVER PEOPLE SIRE
A MESSAGE LEAVES THE FOREST KINGDOM WITH HOPES OF EASING THE BUILDING TENSIONS

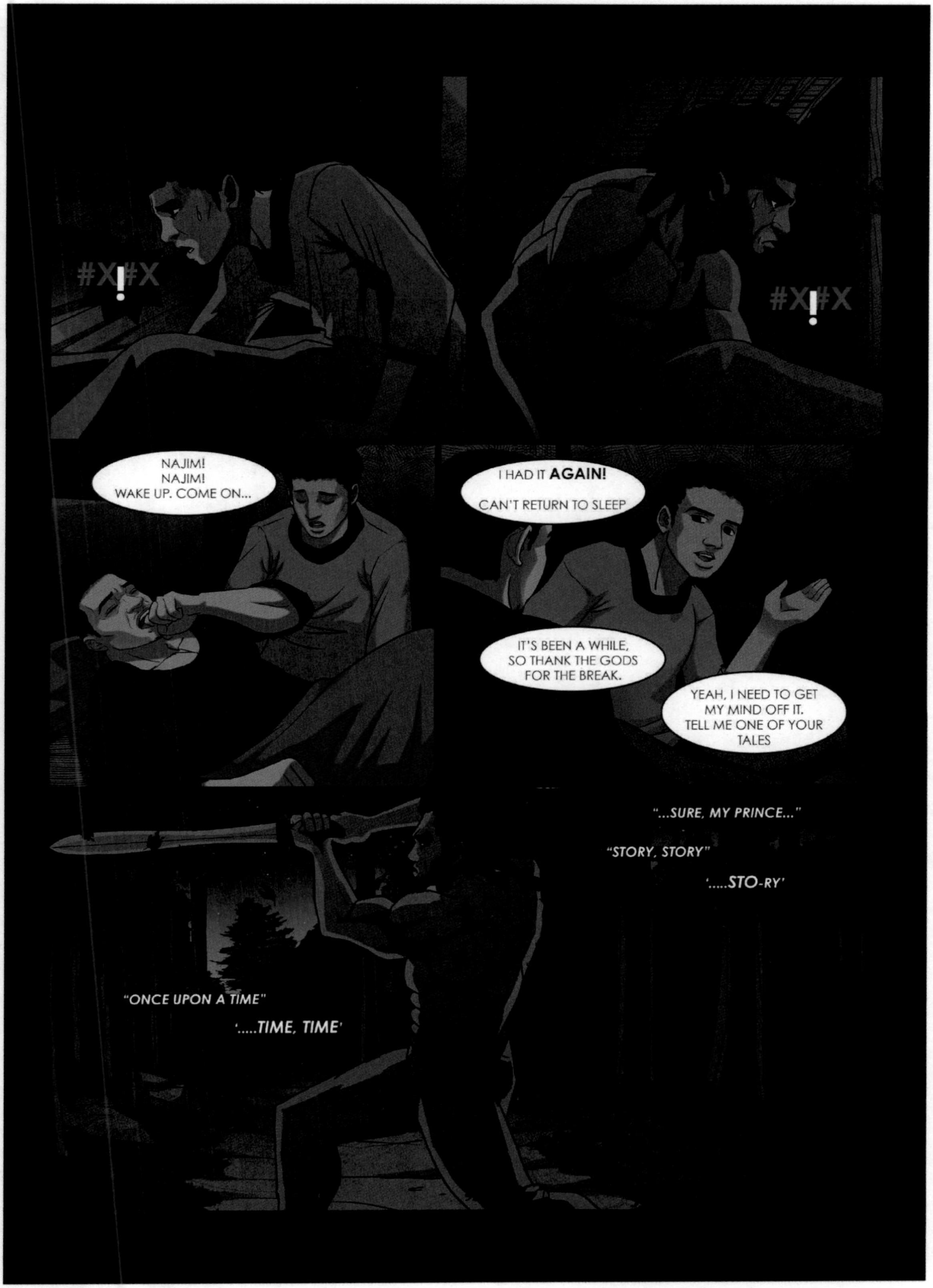
#X!#X
#X!#X
NAJIM! NAJIM! WAKE UP. COME ON...
I HAD IT AGAIN! CAN'T RETURN TO SLEEP
IT'S BEEN A WHILE, SO THANK THE GODS FOR THE BREAK.
YEAH, I NEED TO GET MY MIND OFF IT. TELL ME ONE OF YOUR TALES
"...SURE, MY PRINCE..."
"STORY, STORY"
'.....STO-RY'
"ONCE UPON A TIME"
'.....TIME, TIME'

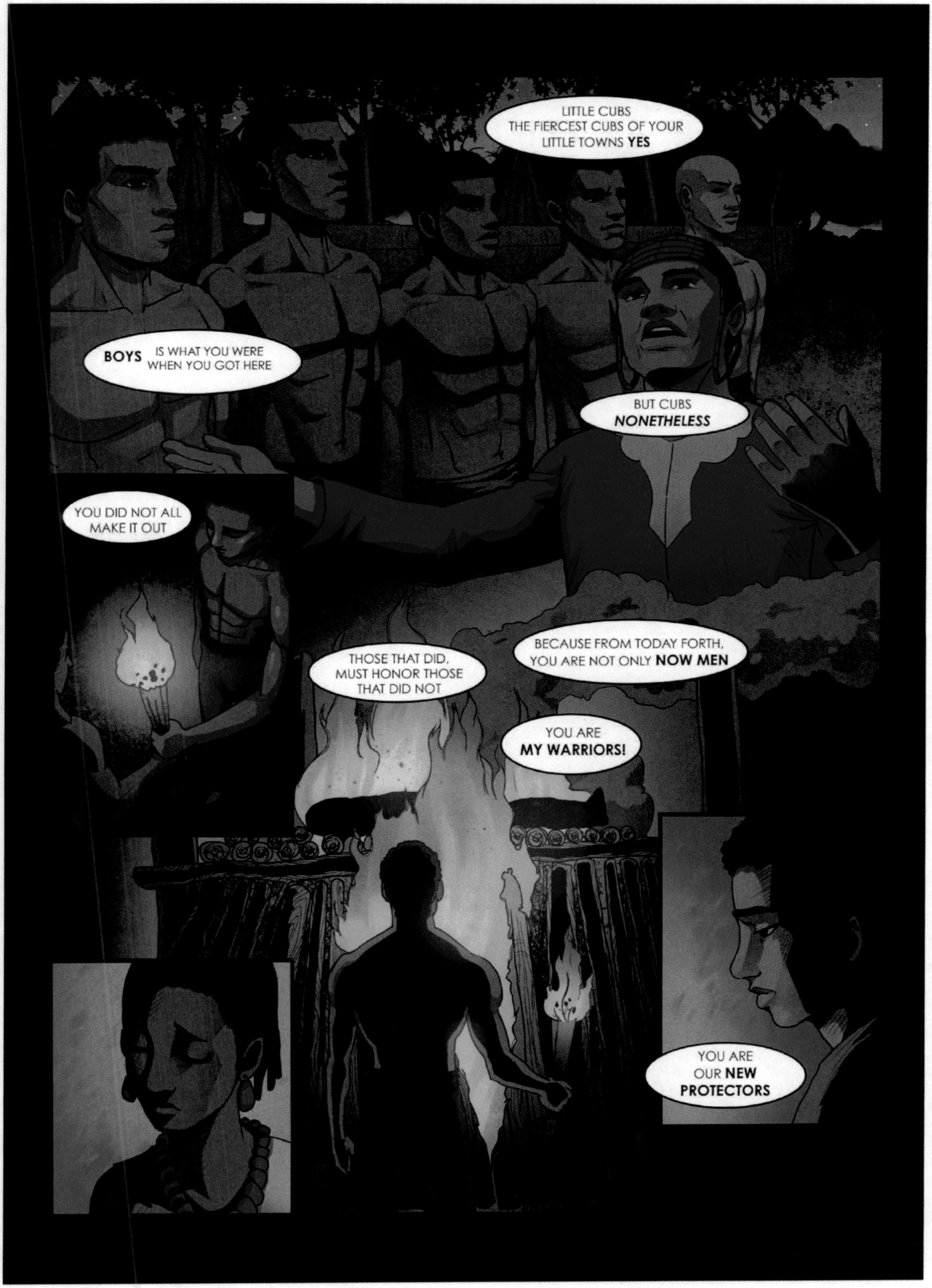
LITTLE CUBS
THE FIERCEST CUBS OF YOUR LITTLE TOWNS YES
BOYS IS WHAT YOU WERE WHEN YOU GOT HERE
BUT CUBS NONETHELESS
YOU DID NOT ALL MAKE IT OUT
THOSE THAT DID, MUST HONOR THOSE THAT DID NOT
BECAUSE FROM TODAY FORTH, YOU ARE NOT ONLY NOW MEN
YOU ARE MY WARRIORS!
YOU ARE OUR NEW PROTECTORS

YOU SAVED ME
*KOFF**CHOKE*
#WHEEZE#........
...FINALLY...

PLEASE MY FRIEND, SAVE YOUR
STRENGTH.
WE'LL GET YOU BACK

RECRUIT WOLE NEVER MET HIS FATHER.
PAPA WOLE WAS BANISHED FOR REASONS NO
ONE SHARED WITH THE YOUNG BOY

HIS VERY BEAUTIFUL MOTHER WAS FORCED TO
MARRY AN UNWORTHY MAN TO SAVE HER VIRTUE
WITHIN THE SOCIETY

A NEED TO UNDO THE SHAME CAUSED BY HIS FATHER

NEEDLESS TO SAY, HE GREW UP WITH
A NEED TO SUCCEED

BUT MOST IMPORTANTLY,
A NEED TO MAKE HIS MOTHER PROUD...

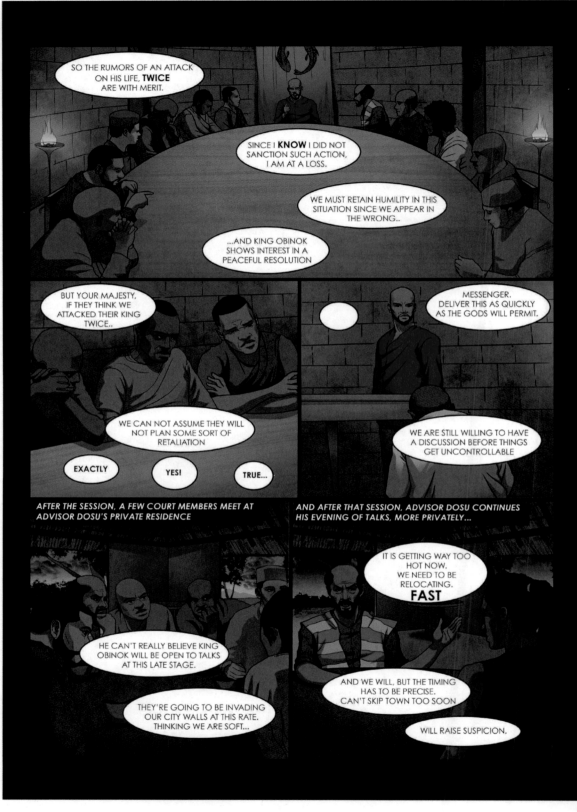

ONCE AGAIN, KING OBINOK'S COURT
PROTECTOR OF THE FOREST KINGDOMS, KING OBINOK
A MESSENGER FOR YOU FROM THE RIVERLANDS
NOW THAT'S A SWIFT MESSAGE IF I EVER SAW ONE.
KING OBINOK
YOUR HIGHNESS
I BRING A MESSAGE FROM KING KINLAY OF THE RIVER KINGDOMS
DELIVER YOUR MESSAGE
HMM, I SEE. WELL, THAT'S PRETTY INTERESTING.
NOURISH YOURSELF MESSENGER, WE WILL PREPARE A RESPONSE.
NOW LEAVE US.

MistryKiDD
Practice Sheet
SEPTEMBER 2010

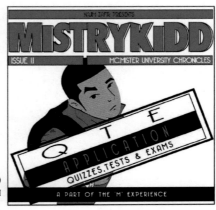

MistryKiDD
Application
APRIL 2011

MistryKiDD
BabyFace Monsta
MARCH 2013

MistryKiDD
Blood Of A Writer
JUNE 2015

Elton Thomasi

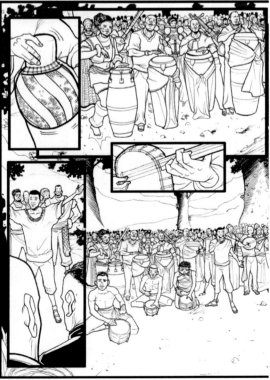